MILITARY JOBS

ARMY RANGERS

What It Takes to Join the Elite

ALEXANDER STILWELL

Cavendish Square
New York

Published in 2015 by Cavendish Square Publishing, LLC
243 5th Avenue, Suite 136, New York, NY 10016

First edition

Website: cavendishsq.com

This publication represents the opinions and views of the author based on his or her personal experiences, knowledge, and research. The information in this book serves as a general guide only. The author and publisher have used their best efforts in preparing this book and disclaim liability rising directly or indirectly from the use and application of this book.

CPSIA compliance information: Batch #WW15CSQ.

All websites were available and accurate when this book was sent to press.

Library of Congress Cataloging-in-Publication Data

Stilwell, Alexander.
Army Rangers: What it Takes to Join the Elite / Alexander Stilwell.
pages cm. — (Military jobs)
Includes index.
ISBN 978-1-50260-166-7 (hardcover) ISBN 978-1-50260-167-4 (ebook)
1. United States. Army. Ranger Regiment, 75th—Juvenile literature. 2. United States. Army—Commando troops—Juvenile literature. I. Title.

UA34.R36S75 2014
356'.1670973—dc23

2014022796

For Brown Bear Books Ltd:
Editorial Director: Lindsey Lowe
Managing Editor: Tim Cooke
Children's Publisher: Anne O'Daly
Design Manager: Keith Davis
Designer: Lynne Lennon
Picture Manager: Sophie Mortimer

Picture Credits:
T=Top, C=Center, B=Bottom, L=Left, R=Right

Front Cover : FC All images Library of Congress
All images © Library of Congress, except; 10, © Bettmann/Corbis; 30, © Shutterstock.

Manufactured in the United States of America

CONTENTS

INTRODUCTION

The 75th Ranger Regiment is one of the world's leading elite units. It is a key part of the U.S. Army Special Operations Command (USASOC).

The U.S. Rangers are a highly mobile light infantry regiment. There are about 2,300 highly trained Rangers, split into three battalions. They are trained for any environment. Their specialty is direct action (DA)—fast, offensive strikes against the enemy.

When Rangers deploy, they get priority over other units, apart from other special forces. They work closely with special forces such as Delta Force and 160th Special Operations Aviation Regiment (SOAR).

Rangers are trained to infiltrate the operational field by land, sea, or air at a few hours' notice. They can exist without other military support for five days. As well as rapid strike missions, the Rangers are experts in urban warfare and also carry out reconnaissance duties and rescue missions.

An Army Ranger keeps a careful lookout during an exercise in urban fighting.

RIGHT FEED

HISTORY

The U.S. Army Rangers owe their name to Rogers' Rangers. In the French and Indian War (1754–63), Rogers' Rangers were frontiersmen who acted as scouts. The Army Rangers were created in World War II (1939–45) as a version of the British Commandos.

U.S. Rangers wait anxiously as their landing craft nears Omaha Beach during the D-Day invasions of France on June 6, 1944.

The Rangers fought on the Normandy beaches during the D-Day landings in June 1944. They scaled a cliff on Omaha Beach to seize a German gun position. In Burma, a Ranger unit known as Merrill's Marauders made a 1,000-mile

U.S. Ranger marksmen keep watch from an observation post during the Korean War.

(1,600-km) march over the Himalaya mountains in order to cut off Japanese forces.

Vietnam and Later

Ranger units served during the Korean War (1950–53) and in the Vietnam War (1964–75). In Vietnam, Long Range Patrol units penetrated into enemy territory. The soldiers who carried out these patrols were formed into Ranger companies. At the end of each of these conflicts, the Rangers were disbanded. However, that all changed in 1974, when the first permanent Ranger battalions were created: 1st, 2nd, and 3rd Battalions (Ranger), 75th Infantry. The 75th Ranger Regiment formally came into existence in February 1986. Today it is based at Fort Benning, Georgia.

EYEWITNESS

"Let the enemy come till he's almost close enough to touch. Then let him have it and jump out and finish him with your hatchet."

—Rangers' Standing Orders, Robert Rogers

THE RANGER CREED

The Ranger creed is the official mission statement of the Rangers. It was written in 1974. Today, all Rangers learn the creed. The first letter of each paragraph spells out the word "Ranger."

The creed lays down the values by which Rangers try to live. Rangers often recite it when they are together on parades.

Reciting the creed often helps build team spirit among units.

Recognizing that I volunteered as a Ranger, fully knowing the hazards of my chosen profession, I will always endeavor to uphold the prestige, honor, and high esprit de corps of my Ranger Regiment.

Acknowledging the fact that a Ranger is a more elite Soldier who arrives at the cutting edge of battle by land, sea, or air, I accept the fact that as a Ranger my country expects me to move further, faster, and fight harder than any other soldier.

Ranger candidates recite the Ranger Creed during a pre-Ranger course in Iraq in July 2011.

Never shall I fail my comrades. I will always keep myself mentally alert, physically strong, and morally straight, and I will shoulder more than my share of the task, whatever it may be, one hundred percent and then some.

Gallantly will I show the world that I am a specially selected and well-trained soldier. My courtesy to superior officers, neatness of dress, and care of equipment shall set the example for others to follow.

Energetically will I meet the enemies of my country. I shall defeat them on the field of battle, for I am better trained and will fight with all my might. Surrender is not a Ranger word. I will never leave a fallen comrade to fall into the hands of the enemy and under no circumstances will I ever embarrass my country.

Readily will I display the intestinal fortitude required to fight on to the Ranger objective and complete the mission, though I be the lone survivor.

WHAT IT TAKES

To become an Army Ranger you need to go above and beyond standard military requirements. You'll need oustanding physical fitness, endurance, stamina, mental toughness, and intelligence.

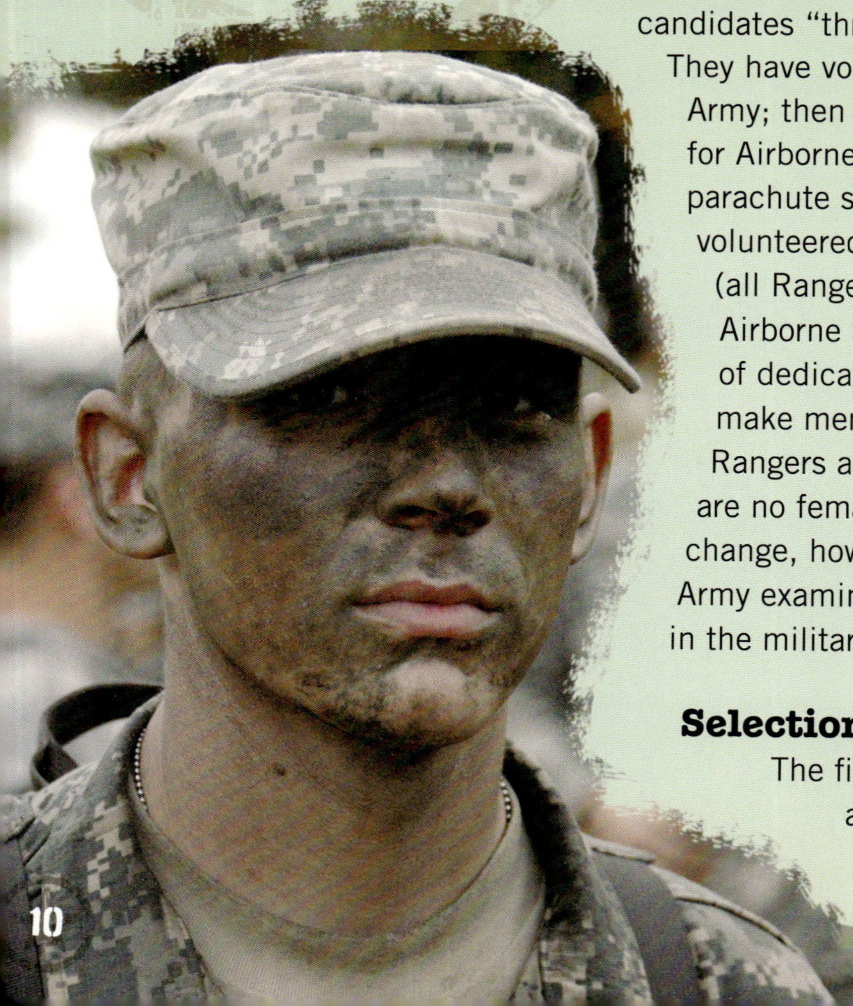

Ranger candidates are already members of the armed forces.

Becoming an Army Ranger is not easy. The Rangers call their candidates "three-time" volunteers. They have volunteered to join the Army; then they have volunteered for Airborne School to learn parachute skills; and they have volunteered to join the Rangers (all Rangers must graduate from Airborne School). It is the sort of dedication that it takes to make men volunteer that the Rangers are looking for. There are no female Rangers. That may change, however, as the U.S. Army examines the role of women in the military.

Selection Procedure

The first stage of becoming a Ranger is the Ranger Assessment and

Soldiers do pull-ups at a U.S. base in Iraq as they prepare to try to become Army Rangers.

Selection Program (RASP). It pushes recruits to test whether they have the toughness to become a Ranger. Recruits prepare for RASP by taking courses to get them fit. Despite this, RASP still has a high drop-out rate.

Ranger School

Recruits who pass RASP join the 75th Ranger Regiment. Then they can go to Ranger School. The school is run by Rangers and trains other military units, too. But all Rangers must pass Ranger School.

IN ACTION

The Ranger target is forty-nine push-ups in two minutes. But these aren't just any push-ups: they're Ranger push-ups. They only count if they are done in the approved way. The chest must touch the ground on every dip, the head has to be up and facing forward, and the push-up must be done slowly.

RANGER ASSESSMENT AND SELECTION PROGRAM

All Rangers must pass the Ranger Assessment and Selection Program (RASP). Even serving Rangers who want to be promoted are expected to pass RASP again.

Ranger candidates move a casualty to a dressing station under enemy fire during a training exercise.

RASP is held at Fort Benning, Georgia. The first phase of the eight-week program lets staff assess which recruits have the staying power to become Rangers. The second phase assesses skills such as marksmanship.

IN ACTION

The third week of RASP begins with "Black Monday." It includes a 12-mile (19-km) road march candidates must complete while carrying a heavy pack. A 50 percent drop-out rate is common.

To the Limits...

In the first phase of RASP, candidates are pushed to the breaking point, both physically and mentally. The most severe part of training comes in the second week. Candidates head to a remote area called Cole Range, where they go through a rigorous series of exercises.

And Beyond

The routine at Cole Range is designed to wear recruits out. They do tedious but demanding tasks, such as push-ups or running sprints. Recruits get an average of only four hours' sleep in the whole week. They are often cold and wet—but must still be able to think clearly.

A candidate reaches out to grasp a rope on an assault course as he tries to qualify for RASP.

GETTING THROUGH RASP

Most candidates drop out during the first phase of RASP. Soldiers who make it to the second phase usually make it through the whole course. They have the mental and physical strength to become Rangers.

To qualify to wear the famous tan beret of the Army Rangers, candidates will have survived the challenges of phase one of RASP. In phase two, they will have been assessed on their ability to operate in small units. They learn techniques such as marksmanship, specialized driving, and getting through defensive perimeters.

Physical Tests

Rangers need exceptional levels of fitness to be effective on active missions. All candidates for RASP have to show that they can pass a series of tough physical tests.

Recruits practice swimming in their uniforms in the pool.

The requirements include:

- 49 push-ups in two minutes
- 59 sit-ups in two minutes
- A minimum of six pull-ups
- A 2-mile (3.2-km) run in under 15 minutes and 12 seconds
- A 5-mile (8-km) run in under 40 minutes
- A 16-mile (26-km) hike with a 65lb (30-kg) pack in under 5 hours and 20 minutes
- A 15-minute swim with equipment.

Candidates move forward across open ground during a small-unit exercise.

Swim Tests

A key part of RASP is the Ranger Swim Ability Evaluation. Candidates are tested on their ability to swim long distances underwater without panicking.

IN ACTION

The reason the Rangers put so much emphasis on swimming skills is that they have to be able to deploy anywhere. Often the best way to infiltrate an operational area is by water, either coming ashore from the sea or moving along rivers. Swimmers are far more stealthy than boats.

RANGER SCHOOL: CRAWL

Once a soldier has passed RASP he can join the 75th Ranger Regiment. He is now a Ranger—but he is not yet the finished article. For that, he still has to survive three demanding phases at Ranger School: "Crawl," "Walk," and "Run."

Recruits jog across a field as a penalty for failing a test at Ranger School.

Rangers on the Crawl Phase rest after a two-hour assault during a combined arms live-fire exercise.

Ranger School was set up to train special forces. It is not just for Rangers, but all Rangers must complete Ranger School.

Crawl Phase

The Crawl phase takes place at Fort Benning. It makes the recruits even fitter. They learn to crawl on ropes through the air and jump into ponds as part of Combat Water Survival Assessment. The Crawl phase also introduces recruits to working in a small combat squad. They learn airborne operations, fieldcraft, and communications.

EYEWITNESS

"Fast-paced instruction on troop leading procedures, principles of patrolling, demolitions, fieldcraft, and basic battle drills focused toward squad ambush and reconnaissance methods."

—Official description of Ranger School: Crawl

RANGER SCHOOL: WALK

The Walk, or Mountain, phase of Ranger School is no place for the faint-hearted. Rangers need a good head for heights, as direct action operations often take them into inhospitable mountain territory.

Mountain ranges are often undefended, so they are potentially a good route into enemy territory. In the 21-day Walk phase of Ranger School, recruits learn the skills they need to operate in mountainous territory. These skills include basic mountaineering techniques, such as tying knots, setting up rope anchors on a cimb, belaying (climbing with ropes), and abseiling down rock faces while carrying heavy packs. Recruits are also taught how to survive in rugged conditions, terrible weather, or when they are tired.

Instructors watch a recruit rappel down a 60-foot (18-m) rock face.

A soldier at Ranger School eats his first hot meal for days while standing up.

Mountain Test

At the end of the Walk phase, the skills the recruits have learned are tested in a series of exercises in mountainous terrain, with rocky peaks, ridges, ravines, and many rivers. The exercises include a four-day combat patrol mission and an air assault in which recruits parachute into a confined space on a mountainside. Recruits also learn how to get any casualties out of the mountains to safety.

EYEWITNESS

"Students are instructed in military mountaineering tasks as well as techniques for employing a squad and platoon for continuous combat patrol operations within a mountainous environment."

—Mir Bahmanyar, former 2/75 Ranger

A recruit has to pass all of the climbing tests if he is to remain on the course. Recruits also have to show that they have the leadership skills and mental agility to plan and lead a combat mission.

RANGER SCHOOL: RUN

The final phase of Ranger School is named "Run." It takes place in the steamy Florida swamps. The recruits learn tropical survival techniques, and practice using weapons in combat.

The coastal swamps of Florida are a challenging environment. They are hot and humid, so any exercise is exhausting. There are many rivers, so recruits learn to use a variety of boats, or to use ropes to cross rivers. The swamps are home to reptiles such as alligators and snakes. Experts teach recruits how to tell poisonous snakes from harmless ones.

Candidates learn how to handle canoes on rivers and lakes.

A Ranger candidate uses a rope to prevent his heavy pack pulling him under as he crosses a river.

EYEWITNESS

"Included in the field training exercises are airborne and helicopter assaults, small boat operations, river crossings, and swamp crossings."

—Official Ranger briefing

Unit Tactics

By the Run phase of Ranger School, the new Rangers are used to working together in small units. In Florida, they continue to work constantly in teams as they plan and carry out raids and ambushes. They also learn to do operations in urban locations.

Island Mission

The final part of the Run phase tests all of the Rangers' skills and teamwork. They have to mount an attack on a well-defended island. It may be an exercise, but it is highly realistic. The recruits have to make their assault against a well-trained "enemy," which consists of experienced Ranger instructors. The recruits have to use their skills in using small boats and their understanding of raiding tactics.

URBAN WARFARE TRAINING

U.S. Army Rangers are specialists in small-unit combat. That means their missions often take them into towns and cities, where terrorists or guerrilla fighters hide among the civilian population.

Street fighting is an intense experience that demands high levels of concentration. In populated areas, the enemy can be hidden anywhere, so Rangers learn how to cover one another as they move through the streets. There are often civilians present. Rangers who come across people must judge quickly whether they are facing an enemy fighter or a noncombatant. Rangers learn Close Quarters Battle (CQB) skills. That improves their reflexes, so that they can decide almost instantly whether to shoot or hold their fire.

A Ranger climbs through a window, having cleared a balcony during a training exercise.

Clearing Buildings

Clearing buildings requires special tactics. Interiors are often dark and smoky, and there is little room for maneuver. Rangers learn how to enter and move through a building while looking out for hidden booby traps. Once inside, they are trained to move as quickly as possible from room to room, so that enemy fighters are taken by surprise and have no time to react.

Special Tactics

Rangers also learn how to apply their marksmanship and sniper skills in an urban environment. They train in keeping up sustained fire against the enemy, even while they are moving through a maze of narrow streets.

EYEWITNESS

"Urban warfare can take many forms ... It is markedly different from combat in a more open or defined theater of operations."

—Report on U.S. military operations, RAND Corporation

Rangers use a smoke bomb for cover as they advance along the side of a building.

HALO JUMPING

All Army Rangers have been to Airborne School to learn how to parachute. Once they become Rangers, they also learn advanced high-altitude jumping.

High-altitude jumping can be very dangerous, especially in High-Altitude Low-Opening (HALO) jumps where Rangers freefall and only open their parachutes at the last moment. The other technique is High-Altitude High-Opening (HAHO).

Secret Insertion

These specialized parachuting techniques are only taught to a select number of U.S. special forces: the Rangers, Delta Force, Marine Corps Force Reconnaissance, and the U.S. Navy SEALs. These are units that often have to get into action quickly and that can operate effectively without much heavy equipment. Parachuting is an ideal way to move Rangers quickly into combat zones.

Rangers leave their aircraft as part of a HALO jump high above a military base in Florida during an air show in 2012.

Rangers jump from an MC-130 Combat Talon II aircraft during a massed jump in 2009.

HALO jumps

HALO jumping was developed to minimize the danger of aircraft and parachutists being detected by the enemy. The airplane flies above enemy radar, and the Rangers open their parachutes as near the ground as possible, when they are under the radar. There is so little oxygen at the start of the jump the Rangers often have to wear oxygen masks.

HAHO jumps

In HAHO jumping, aircraft do not enter enemy airspace. Rangers are dropped from a much greater height and use their Ram Air parachutes to guide themselves into the target area, or drop zone.

IN ACTION

The Ram Air Parachute System (RAPS) is highly maneuverable. It can fly at up to 30 miles per hour (50km/h). It can support 450 pounds (204 kg) of suspended weight.

AIR ASSAULT

As well as parachuting, Airborne School trains Army Rangers to conduct air-assault operations. They use helicopters to land in or to hover just above the drop zone.

Helicopters were first used in warfare in the 1950s in Korea. They are ideal for transporting special forces because they are very maneuverable. They can even drop small groups of soldiers in areas without roads or any flat ground to use as landing strips. When Army Rangers reach their destination, the helicopters often do not land. That cuts down the time they are exposed to enemy fire.

Rangers drop from a Chinook CH-47 during a live-fire exercise near Fort Stewart, Georgia.

Rangers are inserted by Black Hawk helicopter on a mission to Honduras in 1988.

IN ACTION

Army Rangers are capable of fast-roping from the CV-22B Osprey tilt-rotor aircraft as well as from conventional helicopters.

Fast-Roping

The helicopters hover just above the ground while the Rangers exit via the back or side doors. One technique for getting to the ground is fast-roping. A rope is lowered from the helicopter and recruits slide down it. The recruit controls the speed of descent by using the grip of his gloved hands, and pressure from his knees and feet.

Fast-roping is dangerous. There are no safety precautions. It is easy to miss the rope or fall, or be put off balance by the movement of the helicopter. At night, chem lights (glow sticks) are put on the rope to help the Rangers see the rope and its angle to the ground.

COMBAT PATROLS

Like their historical predecessors, Army Rangers are skilled at working in small teams in enemy territory. Combat patrols can reach their targets without being detected, spring a surprise attack, and escape as quickly as they came.

Combat patrols take different forms. They all involve potentially coming into contact with the enemy, so there is always a chance of a sudden firefight. The most defensive kind of patrol is a security patrol, when Rangers cover the perimeters of U.S. positions to make sure they have not been infiltrated.

Army Rangers speed across the water with their weapons at the ready.

A Ranger patrol makes its way through a swamp after leaving their rubber craft. The rules for patrols are laid down in the Standing Orders.

On the Attack

Offensive patrols take the form or raids or ambushes. Rangers launch raids to harass enemy forces, destroy enemy facilities, and to capture enemy soldiers and equipment. The Rangers get into position quickly, so that they can take the enemy by surprise, and they use overwhelming firepower. They move around to confuse the enemy about where they are, or how many of them there are.

Ambush Tactices

Rangers are experts at ambush, when a combat patrol lies in wait to launch a sudden attack on the enemy. The Rangers learn what to do when the signal for an ambush is given. All instructions are given with arm and hand signals, in order to avoid alerting the enemy.

EYEWITNESS

"Don't ever march the same way. Take a different route so you won't be ambushed."

—Standing Orders, Rogers' Rangers

MOUNTAIN WARFARE

Mountains are some of the most hostile terrain on Earth. But they are militarily vital. It's easy for the enemy to hide in mountain ranges. Mountain peaks also provide good observation points and make it difficult for an enemy to counterattack.

In recent U.S. Army operations, the Rangers have served in mountainous countries such as Afghanistan. Mountains present huge challenges, including severe and unpredictable weather conditions.

Rangers move across a rock slope in the foothills as they train for mountain combat.

Rangers use optical sights to watch for enemy movement on the flat lands beneath their mountainous observation point.

The Rangers need all the climbing skills they have learned at Ranger School. Among the techniques they use are climbing and mountain walking, constructing bridges and shelters, skiing and walking on snow and ice, and mountain rescue.

Traveling Light

One advantage the Rangers have in mountainous terrain is that they are trained to travel light. They are used to operating effectively without vehicles or artillery.

IN ACTION

On lower slopes and rugged terrain, only basic mountaineering skills are necessary. Steeper slopes may require fixed ropes and the use of assault climbers. On near-vertical cliff faces, only specialized assault climbers have the required technical expertise.

TROPICAL WARFARE

Rangers get a good taste of tropical warfare in the Run phase of Ranger School, when they carry out operations in the steamy Florida swamps.

The Florida section of Ranger School prepares recruits for conditions in the tropical jungle.

Tropical warfare challenges soldiers like few other sorts of warfare. It is a specialty of U.S. special forces, because it is so demanding. The thick vegetation in the jungle means that the enemy might be hiding only a few feet away. Rangers learn how to turn the jungle to their advantage by using camouflage to conceal their own positions.

U.S. Rangers pause while making a patrol during jungle survival training.

Survival Skills

Rangers learn survival skills such as how to create shelters off the ground to avoid venomous reptiles and insects, and how to deal with the constant humidity. They also learn how to find their way through the thick vegetation. Other key skills include tracking animals and reading their behavior. Army Rangers are trained in advanced reconnaissance skills and jungle movement techniques that allow them to locate enemy positions without being discovered.

EYEWITNESS

"The jungle environment includes densely forested areas, grasslands, cultivated areas, and swamps. Jungles are classified as primary or secondary jungles based on the terrain and vegetation."

—U.S. Army Field Manual

DESERT OPERATIONS

Deserts cover about a third of the world's land surface—more than any other climate zone. They include regions that control the world's oil supply. These locations have seen intense conflict in recent years—and may do so again in the future.

The desert has little cover from the blazing sun, but at night the temperate may drop by as much as 70 degrees. It is so cold that Rangers risk hypothermia as much as sunstroke and dehydration. Visibility falls from about 30 miles (50 km) on a clear day to little over 30 feet (9 m) in a thick sandstorm.

Rangers on a training patrol in desert conditions in Iraq.

Ranger candidates find any cover they can during ambush training in the Nevada desert.

Desert Survival

Army Rangers are trained to acclimatize to the desert environment as quickly as possible. They learn that their priority is to find sources of water and to conserve the water they have. They also need to build shelters to protect them from the sun during the day and provide warmth during the night. Wearing hats, scarves, or face masks protects the head and face from the sun and the effects of blown sand. Sunglasses help to reduce the glare of the sun reflected off the desert floor.

Because desert environments are often flat and open, Rangers learn to conceal themselves among rocks and vegetation so that they are hidden from the enemy. This allows them to carry out reconnaissance duties without being detected.

IN ACTION

The key to desert survival is water. In order to combat water loss and remain hydrated in a desert with an average temperature of 95°F (35°C), Rangers need to drink at least 1 gallon (4 liters) of water every twenty-four hours. If they are active, they need to drink even more.

AIRCRAFT

U.S. Army Rangers use a variety of fixed-wing airplanes and helicopters. They are trained to carry out both parachute drops and air assaults. Either way, air power is essential to get the Rangers into the areas where they are needed.

The advantage of airplanes for the Rangers is that they can move large numbers of men over long distances. The MC-130J Commando II is a special operations version of the C-130 Hercules transport aircraft. The MC-130J is used for delivering special forces to missions, retrieving them afterward, and resupplying them in between. It is also capable of refuelling

A C-17 Globemaster takes off from a base in Afghanistan. For a large aircraft, it can use very short landing strips.

Rangers board an MC-130 Hercules aircraft before a parachute jump.

special operations helicopters such as the MH-60M Black Hawk. A Combat Systems Officer (CSO) onboard uses radar and other systems to keep Rangers on the ground updated about exactly what's going on around them.

C-17 Globemaster

The C-17 gives Rangers the ability to move a lot of men quickly. The aircraft can carry 102 paratroopers at 515 mph (830 km/h). It can land on an airstrip as short as 3,500 feet (1,060 m).

IN ACTION

The Boeing V-22B Osprey is a tilt-rotor aircraft. It has the advantages of an airplane and a helicopter. It can carry twenty-four combat troops at twice the speed of a helicopter, but it can land vertically, so it can drop and pick up Rangers in a limited space.

HELICOPTERS

The helicopter is key to many Army Ranger operations. Helicopters can get Rangers into all sorts of combat positions, even in towns or cities.

An MH-6M Little Bird helicopter lands Rangers on roof tops during an urban combat exercise.

The Rangers use a range of different helicopters. The MH-47G Chinook is a heavy-lift aircraft that has been specially adapted for special operations with increased armor and firepower. It is flown by the 160th Special Operations Aviation Regiment (SOAR). The MH-60M Black Hawk is a special version of the UH-60 helicopter. The Black Hawk is fitted with

An MH-60M Black Hawk helicopter drops Rangers into a lake at the start of a mission.

state-of-the-art day and night optics, multi-mode radar with all-weather capability, enhanced integrated weapons systems, and new high-performance engines. It can also reach higher altitudes than previous versions. This helicopter is useful for dangerous special operations work because of its rugged crash-proof design.

MH-6M Little Bird

The MH-6M is also known as the Mission Enhanced Little Bird. It is an advanced special operations helicopter. It is used on missions such as forward air control and infiltration and extraction. With a crew of two, the agile helicopter has outside benches to carry three Rangers on each side. The Little Bird is small enough to fly between buildings and to land Army Rangers on rooftops for urban combat.

IN ACTION

Special forces helicopters are adapted to carry out long-range missions at low level, by day or night, and in adverse weather. They have features such as terrain-following radar and forward-looking infrared (FLIR), which also help navigation.

GROUND MOBILITY VEHICLE

For ground operations, the Rangers use a special forces version of the Humvee (the High Mobility Multipurpose Wheeled Vehicle).

The new vehicle is known as the Ground Mobility Vehicle–Ranger (GMV-R). A number of features distinguish it from the standard Humvee. These include a more powerful engine, an open-bed rear for easy storage of equipment, a Global Posititioning System (GPS) navigation

A Ranger fires a machine gun mounted on top of a Special Operations Vehicle.

The GMV-R has rugged tires and high ground clearance, so it can cross the roughest terrain.

system, greater ground clearance for rugged terrain, tougher suspension, and more rugged tires.

Armored Vehicle

The GMV-R has weapons mounts that can turn it into a bristling gunship. It can carry different calibers of machine gun, including heavy belt-fed machine guns, as well as 40mm grenade launchers.

IN ACTION

The GMV-R has adaptations that make it ideal for operations in enemy territory. It has a winch to tow broken-down vehicles. It also has smoke-grenade launchers. These can be used to create an instant smokescreen while breaking away from the enemy.

MOGADISHU

From August 22, 1993, Task Force Ranger was deployed to Somalia in West Africa. Its target was General Mohamed Farah Aideed, a warlord in a civil war that had been raging since the 1980s.

The Task Force included members of Delta Force, the U.S. Navy SEALs, and Army Rangers. They planned to capture Aideed's lieutenants at a hotel in the capital, Mogadishu, on October 3, 1993. The raiding party included about seventy-five Rangers and forty Delta Force soldiers.

Rangers ride into Mogadishu on a Black Hawk helicopter during U.S. operations in Somalia.

A U.S. helicopter flies above the Somali capital, Mogadishu.

Disastrous Raid

The Rangers arrived in Black Hawk helicopters while Delta Force soldiers approached in Little Bird helicopters. A Ranger ground force arrived, but it came under fire, and a Black Hawk was also shot down.

A combat search and rescue team (CSAR) arrived, but its helicopter was shot down.The Rangers had to fight their way to safety. The Task Force suffered sixteen dead and twelve wounded. Aideed lost about 1,000 men, but the raid was a failure.

EYEWITNESS

"Helicopter gunships were being used as well as all sorts of automatic weapons on the ground by the U.S. and the United Nations. The Somalis, by and large, were using automatic rifles and grenade launchers and it was a very nasty fight, as intense as any battle you would find."

—Robert B. Oakley, U.S. Representative in Somalia

TAKUR GHAR

The 75th Ranger Regiment was heavily engaged in the battle against Taliban and al-Qaeda fighters in the mountains of southern Afghanistan. In March 2002 they tried to occupy the peak of Takur Ghar as an observation post.

Rangers in Afghanistan were armed with SAW machine guns.

A U.S. Navy SEAL team was airlifted to Takur Ghar, but Taliban on the mountain fired on their helicopter. One of the SEALs fell out of the helicopter, which crash-landed a few miles away. Another SEAL team flew in, but came under heavy fire. A Ranger Quick Reaction Force (QRF) was called in, but their helicopter was also shot down by enemy fire.

No Man Left Behind

Three Rangers died, but the rest got out of the crashed helicopter and defended their position. They were soon joined by more Rangers who had landed further down the hill. The Rangers called in air strikes as they attacked the enemy. They soon took command of the hill, although Taliban fighters continued to fire on them from a distance. The Ranger team was extracted after dark. As their creed states, they had not left any dead or wounded behind.

EYEWITNESS

"Everyone kind of moved from a seated position to a kneeling position, and made sure their muscles were ready to run, to shoot, to dive, to crawl—whatever they needed to do when they hit the ground."

—Ranger Captain Nate Self, Quick Reaction Force

The mountains of Afghanistan were tough terrain for armed combat.

GLOSSARY

abseil To descend a rock face by sliding down ropes.

ambush A suprise attack by people who are lying in wait.

avionics Electronic equipment fitted inside an aircraft.

belay To fix ropes to pins for rock-climbing.

camouflage To use colors or materials to make something blend with the surroundings.

combined arms Military exercises that involve more than one branch of the armed services, such as the Army and the Air Force.

creed A set of beliefs that affects how a person behaves.

fieldcraft The techniques needed to survive in the field, especially without being discovered by the enemy.

hyperventilate To breathe uncontrollably quickly.

infiltrate To move into position for an operation without being spotted by the enemy.

infrared An invisible form of electromagnetic waves.

navigation The act of finding out one's geographical location and planning a route.

noncombatants Civilians who are not engaged in the fighting in a war.

operational area The location where a mission takes place.

rappel To slide quickly down a rope.

reconnaissance To use observation to find out about an enemy's positions.

reflex action An automatic reaction to a situation or event.

scout A soldier who moves ahead of a main force to gather information about an area or about the enemy.

sniper A marksman who shoots at people from a hidden position.

tilt-rotor An aircraft that combines wings with rotors, so it is more maneuverable than an airplane.

FURTHER INFORMATION

BOOKS

Besel, Jennifer M. *The Army Rangers.* Elite Miltary Forces. North Mankato, MN: First Facts Books, 2011.

Gordon, Nick. *Army Rangers.* US Military. Minneapolis, MN: Bellwether Media, 2012.

Lusted, Marcia Amidon. *Army Rangers: Elite Operations.* Military Special Ops. Minneapolis, MN: Lerner Publications, 2013.

Rose, Simon. *Army Rangers.* US Armed Forces. New York, NY: AV2 by Wiegl, 2013.

Sandler, Michael. *Army Rangers in Action.* Special Ops. New York, NY: Bearport Publishing, 2008.

Vanderhoof, Gabrielle, and C.F. Earl. *Army Rangers.* Special Forces: Protecting, Building, Teaching, and Fighting. Broomall, PA: Mason Crest Publishers, 2010.

WEBSITES

www.army.mil/ranger
The official website of the U.S. Army Rangers, with videos and features.

science.howstuffworks.com/army-ranger.htm
Pages on the Rangers from Howstuffworks.com.

www.ranger.org
The U.S. Army Ranger Association, with articles about Ranger history.

www.military.com/special-operations/joining-the-army-rangers.html
Military.com site about training to become an Army Ranger.

Publisher's note to educators and parents: Our editors have carefully reviewed these websites to ensure that they are suitable for students. Many websites change frequently, however, and we cannot guarantee that a site's future contents will continue to meet our high standards of quality and educational value. Be advised that students should be closely supervised whenever they access the Internet.

INDEX